For the hundreds (count 'em!) of friends who helped me
launch Juicy Joy. Hundreds of hugs to you all! —L.M.

For the new readers—
Happy 100th Day! —C.M.

Text copyright © 2010 by Lisa McCourt.
Illustrations copyright © 2010 by Cyd Moore.

Library of Congress Cataloging-in-Publication Data

McCourt, Lisa.
  It's the 100th day, Stinky Face! / by Lisa McCourt ; illustrated by
Cyd Moore.
     p. cm. -- (Scholastic reader. Level 1)
  "Cartwheel Books."
  Summary: Mama helps Stinky Face discover one hundred things he can
bring to school that are special to him.
  ISBN-13: 978-0-545-11509-4
  ISBN-10: 0-545-11509-4
  [1. Mother and child--Fiction. 2. Questions and answers--Fiction. 3.
Hundredth Day of School--Fiction.] I. Moore, Cyd, ill. II. Title. III.
Title: It is the 100th day, Stinky Face. IV. Title: It's the one
hundredth day, Stinky Face.
  PZ7.M47841445Iss 2010
   [E]--dc22
                          2008033407

                  ISBN 978-0-545-11509-4

10 9 8 7 6 5 4 3 2 1   10 11 12 13 14 15/0

            Printed in the U.S.A.   40 • First printing, December 2010

It's the 100th Day, Stinky Face!

by Lisa McCourt
illustrated by Cyd Moore

Cartwheel
·B·O·O·K·S·®

SCHOLASTIC INC.

New York   Toronto   London   Auckland
Sydney   Mexico City   New Delhi   Hong Kong

On the 100th Day of School,
I have to bring 100 somethings.
So I have a question.

Mama, can I bring 100 balloons to school?

Good idea. Except they might
lift you up and fly you away.

What if I brought
100 stars from the sky?

Or . . . we could *draw* 100 stars.

Sorry. Not the same.
Can I bring 100 hamsters?
Good idea. Too bad Rylie is allergic.

Mama, do you think I could get 100 butterflies to land on me?

If you could, you'd be all set!

But, Mama, some of them would probably fly away before I got to school.

Probably.

What if I turned into a
monster and grew 100 teeth?

Oooooh, you could really crunch up those 100th Day snacks then.

December
10

January
5

Why don't you bring 100 stickers?

Or 100 beads?

Or 100 pennies?

But, Mama, those things aren't special to ME. What should I bring, Mama? What should I bring?

So many questions!

That's it, Mama! I'll bring my questions!

But, how will you show your questions to the class?

I'll make a question mark for every question I've asked today! But, Mama, do you think I've asked 100?

I do, my Stinky Face.
I really do!